if you want
to see a

for clio rose —j.f.

*for katie, who would want to see a whale
with me (or a dolphin) —e.s.*

Text copyright © 2013 by Julie Fogliano
Illustrations copyright © 2013 by Erin E. Stead
A Neal Porter Book
Published by Roaring Brook Press
Roaring Brook Press is a division of Holtzbrinck Publishing Holdings Limited Partnership
175 Fifth Avenue, New York, New York 10010
mackids.com
All rights reserved

Library of Congress Cataloging-in-Publication Data

Fogliano, Julie.
If you want to see a whale / Julie Fogliano ; Erin E. Stead. — 1st ed.
    p. cm.
"A Neal Porter Book."
    Summary: Advises the reader about what to do, and not do, in order to
successfully spot a whale, such as wrapping up in a not-too-cozy blanket,
ignoring the roses, and especially, being patient.
    ISBN 978-1-59643-731-9 (hardcover)
[1. Whale-watching—Fiction. 2. Patience—Fiction.] I. Stead, Erin E.,
ill. II. Title.
    PZ7.F6763If 2013
    [E]—dc23
                                                    2012012988

Roaring Brook Press books are available for special promotions and premiums.
For details contact: Director of Special Markets, Holtzbrinck Publishers.

First edition 2013
Book design by Jennifer Browne and Philip C. Stead
Printed in China by South China Printing Co. Ltd., Dongguan City, Guangdong Province

10 9 8 7 6 5 4 3 2 1

if you want
to see a whale

words by julie fogliano
pictures by erin e. stead

A NEAL PORTER BOOK
ROARING BROOK PRESS
NEW YORK

if you want to see a whale
you will need a window

and an ocean

and time for waiting

and time for looking

and time for wondering "is that a whale?"

and time for realizing "no, it's just a bird"

if you want to see a whale
you will need a not-so-comfy chair
and a not-too-cozy blanket
because sleeping eyes can't watch for whales
and whales won't wait for watching

if you want to see a whale
you'll have to just ignore the roses
and all their pink
and all their sweet
and all their wild and their waving
because roses don't want you watching whales
or waiting for
or wondering about
things that are not pink
and things that are not sweet
and things that are not roses

if you want to see a whale
don't look way out and over there
to the ship that is sailing
with the flag that is flapping

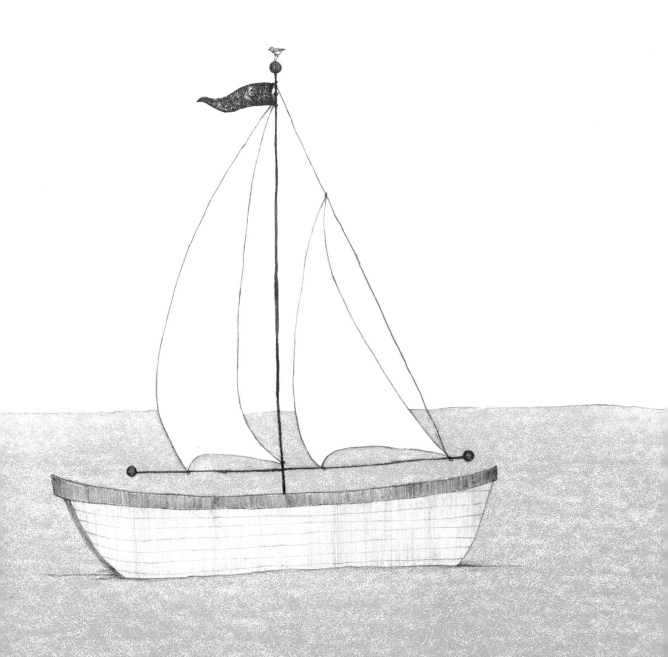

because possible pirates won't help at all
when you're waiting for a whale

if you want to see a whale
there's no time to watch the pelican
who may or may not be smiling
while sitting, staring, looking out
because pelicans who sit and stare can never be a whale

if you want to see a whale
be careful not to notice
something inching, small and green
across the leaf, just nibble scoot
because things that are smaller than most small things
can't be as giant as a whale

if you want to see a whale
you shouldn't watch the clouds
some floating by, some hanging down
in the sky that's spread out, side to side
or the certain sun that's shining
because if you start to look straight up
you might just miss a whale

if you want to see a whale
keep both eyes on the sea

and wait . . .

and wait . . .

and wait . . .

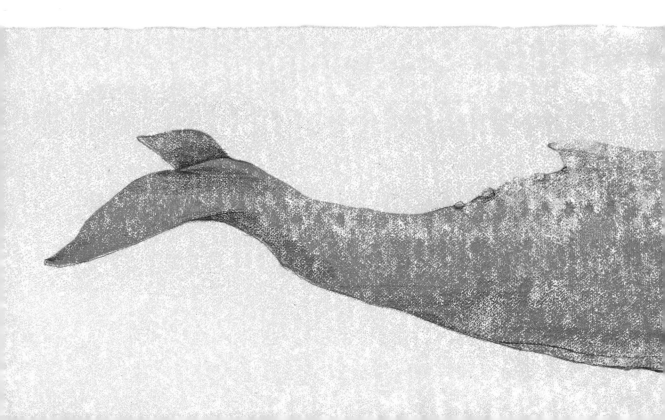

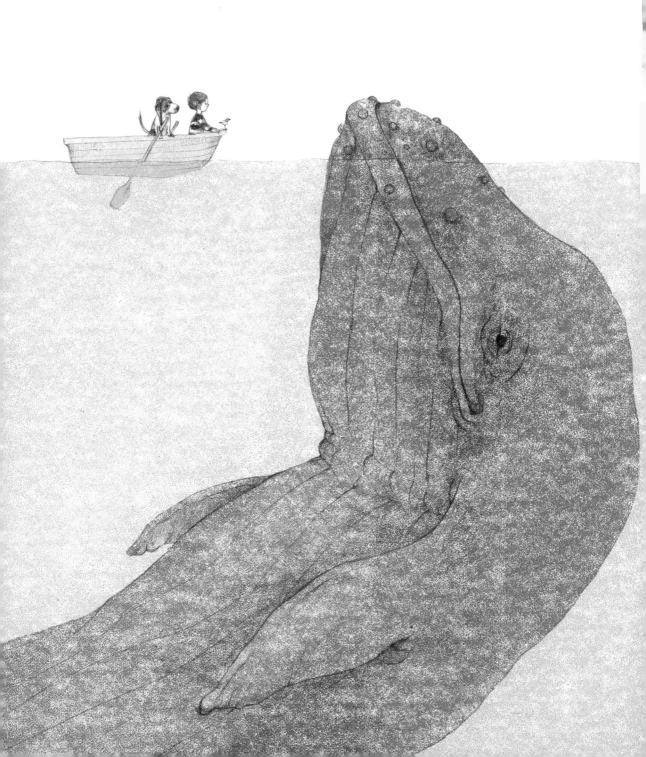